ORED HALL

B.C. Woodruff

Ian Morgenheim

Matt Ewart

Alexandra Graves

JP McGlynn

JD Lyonhart

A WORK FROM SHATTER BOOKS

AN ANTHOLOGY

Table of Contents

V *Foreword*

———

MATT EWART

7 Aimless

JP MC GLYNN

21 Storm Light

ALEXANDRA GRAVES

31 #NoFilter

JD LYONHART

37 Terminal

49 Tits

53 Trump sparks War with CBS

57 3rd Corinthians

B.C. WOODRUFF

61 A Housing Crisis [on Infinite Earths]

67 Doesn't She Look Like Laura Moon?

73 Delight with Destruction

81 Echoes of Us

IAN MORGENHEIM

87 Sixth

———

91 *Contributors*

Foreword

I wrote my first stories over 25 years ago on a Kaypro 4 – a squat, 23-pound beast of a computer that ranked among the most popular PCs of the early 80s. I must have been in first or second grade, which explains but doesn't quite excuse my habit at the time of writing in all caps. While the material itself is gone, the feeling – an almost conspiratorial sense that I was getting away with something – has never quite faded. And now, with no fewer than six contributors making this anthology possible, I think I've finally found my conspiracy. New worlds have a nasty habit of vanishing without scaffolding and support, after all. Score one for the enemies of entropy!

The Mirrored Hall runs the gamut from urban fantasy and science fiction to horror and satire, and I couldn't be more proud of what we've accomplished. Here's to many more.

—IAN MORGENHEIM

Aimless

by Matt Ewart

It was going to be one of those days. Levi could tell already.

The drive home from work was as uneventful as the day that filled it: emails, faxes, Carl complaining about the new IT system, and Emily ending their six year relationship.

That was a bit of an aberration in his usual 9-5.

Driving down the busy, rush-hour-full road, Levi caught glimpses of people living in their own universe – a different page from the same book, connected but never to meet. Probably for the best – they all looked like assholes, thought Levi.

Looking out the window in his cherished 1996 Toyota Camry, the brown cloth seats vibrated in contemptuous synchrony with the engine, which seemed to be experiencing its own existential crisis, trying to free itself from the shackles for which it was designed. Or it needed an oil change. One of the two.

Squirming like some grotesque half robot half human millipede, traffic inched slowly forward. The flickering heat waves protesting the Sun's waxing light, trying to shoo it away. Levi mused on this – he usually didn't have these types of thoughts. Or if he did, he'd turn to Emily and she'd raise an eyebrow mischievously and he'd think of happier thoughts – that's what she did to him. Made him happy.

But that was over, and here he was imagining heatwaves telling the sun to fuck off.

So far, so good.

Summer in LA is not a glorious thing. It's hot, it's smoggy, it's sticky. That's what Levi hated the most about it. The stickiness. It made everything feel wrong. LA heat doesn't make anything flourish, it makes things survivors. Prickly and fiercely protective of what little life they cling on to. Levi thought it did the same to people. Also, it made people wear shorts, which showed off a lot of knee – he always felt they moved the wrong way. He was fully aware that this was a weird thing to believe, but that didn't make him feel any less strongly about it.

As the traffic began to dissipate, he was able to speed up a bit. That felt good – the speed. He had no idea why though, he was racing back to what he could only assume was a ransacked home, with half of their stuff gone, sacrificed to the gods of Divorce. And what angry gods they were. So he was expecting a lot of negative spaces. Emptiness bigger than the objects that held their place.

Levi shook his head, his short hair not moving in the slightest to the movement. He'd need a drink when he got home; it wasn't like him to think like an emotional teenager writing his or her first breakup song over the Key of A minor – not that Levi knew anything about music, but he assumed this was A) a thing, and B) where it all started.

Either way, it felt good to go fast.

The cracked pavement rumbled with the Camry's passing. Deep, resonating bass that protested the awesome power and weight of the car as it continued its journey home.

Crossing over into the valley, the palm trees gave way to

slightly taller palm trees. Costcos and Red Lobsters appeared in the distance, mingling with blocks and blocks of homes. From a distance, they didn't look like much. From up close, the same. Levi lived in one of those unremarkable homes. But that's only because he couldn't afford anything nicer. Not because he liked the unremarkable. Definitely not that.

As Levi pulled into his street, he saw his neighbor, a tiny blonde who he swore used to be on TV, but never bothered asking her. She waved as she planted some kind of tomato or flower in her tiny front garden. Levi raised his fingers off of the steering wheel in response – that was cool, he'd have to do that again.

After putting the beast into park, he opened the car door and stepped out into the muggy-dry-swamp-late-afternoon air. Emily's flowers greeted him as he walked up the concrete path to his beige two story home. They'd die soon, without Emily's protective and nurturing nature. He'd either overwater them, or more likely, completely forget they existed.

He jiggled the lock open, the metal hot to the touch. The door opened. Hesitating, he took a deep breath and walked in. Cool, sweet AC enveloped him, ice dancing away the intruding warm air.

Everything was there. All of their photos, all of her awards, all of her books, all of her everything. Fuck. That meant she'd be coming later to pick that up. Levi didn't know how to feel about that. He did feel, however, that he needed to drink. To excess. To the point of no return. To the point of karaoke.

He walked to the kitchen, still clean and tidy from his deep clean yesterday. God, he loved to clean. Some say it was because it gave him control, and that tidiness was his futile gesture to the absolute power of entropy and, ultimately, death. He actually just didn't want to get sick because fuck bacteria, those little invisible shits.

He found an old bottle of rum in the back of a lesser-used cupboard. It was two thirds full. Oh yeah, he remembered that he got this to make mojitos at his aunt's five year sobriety party. Sometimes Levi had the best intentions but then messed it up with worse actions. Whatever, he had a great time there, despite her shitty catering.

He poured a tall glass of the amber liquid. He took a whiff and recoiled. It smelled angry and cheap and full of sinister promise. Levi smiled and took a long drink.

He sputtered and coughed up half of it.

"Yikes. That looks rough," said a woman.

Levi let out a startled shriek and spun around. There was no one there.

"Who's there?!" He took out a kitchen knife and held it out in what he hoped was threateningly. It hadn't been sharpened in years, but it was the thought that counted. Intentions, once again.

"I think it's just you and me." The voice stated matter of factly.

Levi sliced at the air "Where are you? Who are you? What is going on?"

A pregnant pause filled the air, as the voice considered her response. "I'm not sure, but it looks like you're having a breakdown of some kind."

Levi sprinted through the house, looking for a hidden person and a speaker, something that would held responsible. Hoping that Ashton Kutcher had reprised his seminal role as king punker. Then Levi remembered Ashton was on a new Netflix show. His schedule just would not have allowed for that.

"So you're saying I'm losing it," Levi said to the air.

He went into the living room and sat on one those modern couches that were as uncomfortable to sit on as a Kerouac novel was to read. He dropped the knife on the polished wood coffee table with a clang.

"Well, that's for a seasoned psychologist to determine," came the reply.

"Where are you?" Levi asked the room a second time.

"Why, here of course."

Levi considered this for a second. "Is here... here?"

"Hmm. That's a question of perspective, now, isn't it?"

"Right." Levi then took another pull on the cheap rum, this time not choking on the foul spirit.

"So are you in my head?" he asked again.

The reply came in the form of a low noise. Levi recognized it as a sigh, as if the voice were considering this. After a while, she replied, "No. I don't think so. It's just the two of us here, and I can see you, so I can't be in your head."

He looked around, "How come I can't see you then?"

"That's a great question. I'm not sure. But I can definitely see you."

"Should I call 911? Am I having a stroke?" Levi asked the air.

"Maybe? I'm not a doctor. But I don't think so. Do you smell toast?"

He took a deep breath in, wiggled his nose, and then shook his head.

Levi looked out the window, to the world that made sense. "So why are you here?"

"To help you."

"Oh." He turned his head back to the room. Even with all the craziness going on, looking at Emily's stuff still made him feel that the breakup was still the thing that made the least sense today. His priorities were a little out of whack, he supposed.

Levi sprung off the couch and walked back into the kitchen. He held the bottle of rum, looked at the glass, and determined that he needed all of it, not just the glass. The little guy just didn't have the required depth to fix this problem.

"What help do I need?" he asked the room.

He didn't hear it, but he felt... joy at the question.

"You're in quite serious danger."

He took another drink. He sighed... "Danger?"

He could almost feel the voice nodding excitedly, "Danger."

He motioned to the room and, he guessed, to the world at large. "Who am I in danger from? Myself?"

He felt the contemplation. "Perhaps, and that would add a certain layer of complexity to this issue, but I think at the moment it's outside that is your biggest concern."

"There's nothing outsi–" Levi stopped himself mid-sentence as he glanced back out the window. In the few seconds he'd looked out and then back in, two big black SUV's, Suburbans, actually – wonderful cars – had appeared on the curb outside his house. That in and of itself was alarming, but the eight incredibly large men in black suits was what really did it for Levi. One pulled out a gun. It looked very real – at least he thought it did. Levi didn't have much of a reference point for deadly weapons.

One of the men opened the back door of one of the Suburbans, and a monstrosity stepped out. At least eight feet tall; it was hairy, grey, with tough leathered skin like a bipedal rhino and the face of a mutated UFC champ. In a Brooks Brothers suit. Levi's brain stopped working. It was a troll. It was a fucking troll. Or an ogre. Levi didn't have much of a reference point for those either.

"What in the actual fuck," he whispered.

He sprung off of the couch and ran to the front door, peering through the little peephole. The convex lens offered a wide view of the men, the beast, and their guns approaching the house.

Levi's heart began to beat faster. "The holy fuck is that?! Why do you know they're here? Why are they here? What did I do? I've got, uh, nothing – I don't even have a passport!" Levi rambled, the words tumbling out of his mouth.

The perky voice responded. "The answer to your first question will actually take longer to tell, and by the time I finish explaining, chances are pretty good you'll be dead by then, which would have made my explanation moot and–"

Flapping his hands in anxiety, Levi interrupted, "Jesus, okay, okay. What should I do?"

"Start by locking the door," she instructed.

A booming knock on the door resulted in Levi letting out a muffled shriek as he fumbled for the lock. As he did, the doorknob began to turn. He backed away quickly. Distance was good.

He then ran to the windows and quickly closed the curtains.

"Are those bulletproof?" the voice asked.

"What? Of fucking course not!" he sputtered. Levi didn't handle stress well, and now that the booze was starting to kick in, he felt less and less on top of his own shit.

"Oh. What a shame." She sounded kind of sad.

The glass shattered as bullets tore through the window, the curtains dancing and shaking to the sharp cracks of the guns. They sounded a lot different than in the movies. There were no dings, no whistles, as the bullets flew through the air. Sharp cracks and booming, thunderous notes that he felt more than he heard.

This was some bullshit.

"I think the front door is a bad option now," the voice mused. "Let's try the back."

Levi nodded numbly and army crawled through the living room, through the kitchen, where he saw just how much of a mess the bullets had made. That was going to take forever to clean up.

As he crawled, he lamented how this day was turning out. Tomorrow, he hoped, would eat less of its own ass.

"Where do I go now?" he asked, his voice cracking with stress. Later, when he tells people about this day, he will omit that. His voice will be commanding and decidedly un-crackly, he thought.

"I've arranged a ride for you. There should be a bus coming through the alley now," came the voice. She sounded like she was right beside him now.

Of course it would be a bus.

As he got to the back door, he opened it cautiously. Ah fuck – it was hot outside. He could hear the front door crashing down. Even from here he could hear the deep laboured breath from the troll-goblin-ogre thing. He'd need clarification later on what it was exactly. It roared as it ransacked the house.

His small, square yard reached out into a gravel alley, shared with another row of bland houses, made equally more bland with their lack of gunfire and impossible monsters.

He trampled over more of Emily's flowers as he crawled on his hands and knees through the dirt garden. He wiped the sweat/tears from his eyes. In the retelling it would only be sweat.

At the entrance to the alley, a huge coach bus turned in. White with tinted windows, It rolled to a stop and hissed as the door opened.

With the grace of a sick manatee out of water, Levi rolled over the back fence, altogether forgetting that a door was a few feet to his right.

He flopped on to the gravel with a thud and a gasp. He slowly got to his feet and stumbled the few feet to the waiting bus. He clambered on.

He immediately wished he didn't.

All of the seats, save for a row near the front, were taken out. In the back was a gigantic... throne? Yeah, shit, that was a throne. What was on it though took a few moments for Levi to register.

On that throne sat the biggest person Levi had ever seen. Actually, more like a giant. At least eleven feet tall, and almost as wide as the bus, this man was impossibly muscled and thick. He wore a bearskin as a goddamned shawl. Ancient, painfully green, scouring eyes glanced down at Levi.

Levi waved casually, "Hey."

Play it cool.

"Levi," came the booming reply. If a collapsing mountain had a bizarre three way with a freight train and a thunderstorm, that unlikely union might sound a lot like this guy.

Reeaaaaaaal deep.

It was so deep and powerful in fact that Levi decided to just take a seat, because he didn't quite trust his legs to support him during this particular moment. So he sat cross-legged, like a child, in front of a literal giant.

Today was truly, deeply, profoundly fucked. He'd call in sick tomorrow for sure.

"That's Olgurdin," came the familiar woman's voice. But this time it sounded like she was very much in the room. And indeed she was. She was driving the bloody bus. Uniform and everything.

Levi couldn't quite decide what to do, so he took a deep breath, pinched the bridge of his nose, and promptly fainted.

—

It wasn't the sounds that Levi registered first. It was the smells. Consciousness slowly trickled back into Levi's mind, as a roaring campfire brought back all sorts of associated thoughts and feelings. He felt happy, like he did when responsibilites didn't quite exist. He was thinking of his child-hood – when his dad took him out a few times to the lakes and mountains around near where he grew up. But that happened a long time ago, didn't it?

As Levi's mind began to play catch up to the now, he snapped back to full awareness. That sucked.

He sat upright and took stock of his surroundings. He was in a warehouse, the giant bus parked nearby. A large fire was in the middle of the concrete floor. He wasn't sure if that was safe, but now wasn't the time to figure that one out.

Around the fire were the same people on the bus. Olgurdin and his massive frame stared deeply into the flames, not registering much else, it seemed.

The woman was writing something down into an ancient-looking notebook. She wasn't in a uniform now, but a pair of leather pants and t-shirt with an old punk band on it. Levi hadn't had a good chance to see what she looked like, but now it was evident that her skin had a definite glow. Like, she actually glowed.

From beyond the bus, a staccato sound of hurried high heels echoed through the empty warehouse. Both Olgurdin and the glowing woman – he'd have to ask her name – turned their heads to the noise.

And, because of course it was, Emily emerged from the darkness beyond the fire's glow.

Levi's heart lurched in his chest, and he forgot how to breathe for a moment. Here she was – beautiful, poised, and... different.

"Levi, we need to talk," she said.

And that's it. That's all it took. All of his emotions, all of his confusion, all of the minor trauma of the last twenty-four hours bubbled up, swirled, had no idea where to go – and then decided this would be the perfect time for Super Nap 2.0.

Levi fainted.

Storm Light

by JP Mc Glynn

Storm light.
Different from all other light.
Bright, almost too bright.
Burnt out eyes in the blindness of night.

Possessed with an evil darkness woven through;
a bleached witch's scalp, burning in the half shadows.

An unsettled glow, full of muddied intent.

A lurker peering through the window, watching,
waiting to see if anyone was home.

The smell of a heath was in the air. The animals sensed it and took cover in advance of the first drops. The wind picked up as a coarse haired wolfhound howled like a tormented devil, ready to lash out and save its waxy hide from the not too distant tumult. The rain began, bringing great sheets of wet that ripped and battered the fields. Liquid swaths were blown asunder, to lash a thousand times at once upon the cursed door of Besnard's house.

It was time.

Inside an old thatched-roof cottage, the great bulk of a man heaved himself up from a wrecked chair that was slowly decaying in front of a roaring fireplace – a comfortable perch full of dust and musical old springs. He sighed a long, weighted breath and stood still, staring with soft focus into the flames. A considerable moment passed as his dead father's voice conjured itself into memory: *'Ya git wrap it 7 times. No fuckin 6 or 2 or 11 but 7! Seven to Heaven. Give at plenty o' rope boy; the longer a rope, the bigger a noos then eh?! Thank ah them huge fuckin heeds thems nasty cunts got. Rope need a be big an' fuckin strong! Just like you m'boy'*. He had committed this act well enough to want it over with quickly; before midnight at least, so that he might return home to his heavy bed, covered with a carpet of woolen blankets and pot bellied pillows and drift away alone into the dark.

Half asleep, he reached to the nail atop the side of the door that held an assortment of black skeleton keys. He was the opposite of a waif, all skin and bones – a fat, tall, bearded old man. Bushy, unkempt hair was a dominant feature of his and he was often imposing but never threatening. For the duty that dragged him away into this sinful night, one might easily underestimate his ability to carry out the task. Never had he been known, throughout village nor county, to succumb to weak knees or a nauseous gut. He *always* followed through, and such a reputation hung over him – often at times to distance others from getting too close.

He wrapped himself in a brown oily trench coat, covered his head with a wide brimmed hat, cut from the same cloth, then fished in a wicker basket for a heavy scarf which he tied with the precision of a master craftsman; one quite used to using his hands.

A wrought-iron lamp was procured from above the hall window. Besnard lit it and again stared into the flames. They seemed to call him into the flickering. Like illuminated sirens that knew his deepest wishes and darkest fears, they seduced him. He fell into a complete surrender, moving closer to the warm lips and deep red eyes of the fire goddess.

"Christ bejeysus!" cried Besnard. He stumbled back, almost pulling the side table and an assortment of dusty books down upon him. The lamp hit the floor, shattering most of its glass panels, as the flame quickly snuffed out in the swift descent. Mild pain was apparent, largely in the space above the eyes. The gentle giant had successfully singed off most of his bushy eyebrows and in doing so, had saved himself the trouble of an annual trim. He gently patted the affected area, taking solace in the fact that his weathered skin had been spared the insatiable appetite of the flames. He wondered why on earth he had put his face so close. As he was about to return to his chair to have a pensive breather, the clock over the mantle struck with a chime that seemed both taunting and maddening. It was at this exact moment that the confused old man felt a very palpable shiver. It was as if a formless hovering specter was rising through his legs, gently ascending along the spine and back, swirling and collecting into itself then lightly climbing over one shoulder, unannounced, as a spider might do, to suddenly and forcefully look into the eyes of the victim. Yet there was nothing to see but gently falling pieces of burnt hair making their way from above his eyes to the hardwood floor. For the first time since he could remember, Besnard was *terrified*.

Of exactly what, he had no idea.

The rain was hellish. It came in from the north, blowing sideways. The air was deeply cold and the horses had hidden themselves in the back of the stable. Besnard hurriedly locked his front door as another deep sense of dread hit him. This time, he felt there was someone moving towards him. He snapped his head to the side and strained his eyes to look as far down the road as he could. But all he saw were black trees creaking and swaying. They seemed to worship the night, beckoning in the darkness that was now all around; a presence that most certainly had arrived and was very aware of the man trying to leave.

"Come an Hamish..ya poof ya! Get yer bollocks on a horse and fuck away out!". He thought of singing a pub song, belting it out loud to defy the bogeyman he had conjured in his mind. He then imagined going down to *The Three Legged Mare* after the job was done, where it would be warm, full of good drink and belly laughter. He decided that's what he would do and the incentive was enough to pull him forward and into the stable. He gently coaxed out the stallion and mounted him before the beast could do otherwise. "Cadwaladr!" shouted Besnard as he kicked his muddied heels into the animal's ribs. The name meant *"battle arranger"* and the sound of it, said with great breath and intention, made both horse and rider feel powerful.

The journey ahead wasn't a long one. It was riding into the unknown that caused Besnard to feel terror. The first mile or so was through open fields, where tall stalks of wheat shafts seemed to sway back and forth, like little heads all motioning a unified, ominous 'Nay'. '*Yea*' was his thought, although paltry and deep with hesitation, still enough to keep horse and rider in forward motion. Now came the bog. The rain had saturated it to the point of being a distinct body of water. Besnard knew the higher ground and where remnants of hard turf would still be hidden. Eventually, *The Dubh Forest* would present the final passageway and he'd be clear and into *The Commons.* It was always the forest that proved the most difficult. The locals loved the *auld biddy gossip, the bollocks talk, the fairy legends and the aged lore.* Even Besnard, after a few pints, started to believe it himself. But nothing ever happened. At least not to him, nor his friends or relations. It was all a load of shite as far as he was concerned. It was entering the clearing near the tallest of the black oak trees that was the thing. It appeared like an abyss; an abyss devoid of all light. *"Once you were in, sure you'd be grand and away with the hack!"* said Father O' Suillebhain from Our Lady of the Perpetual Sorrows. Besnard had never heard it confirmed that the Father had ever entered the forest himself, let alone knew his way around a steed. "Bollocks to the Church!"

shouted the bulky man as he lurched himself and horse forward into the pitch-black woods.

The darkness can be comforting when you know you're safe. It's when evil is hiding that the mind conjures the most terrible of ideas, many of which could definitely come true.

It was not more than a few hard minutes ride to get from the clearing to The Commons. It now appeared as though *time itself had slit its own throat.* He had a clear thought of very red, warm thick blood, pouring freely from the gaping wound; the more it bled, the slower reality seemed to move. The horse galloped as if in a dream. A canter now felt like a trot except the stallion leapt with great force over fallen branches and holes, still sweating, snorting and heaving, but all of it was in a drawn-out state of motion. Besnard was sure he may be drunk but he hadn't touched a drop for days. The beast now seemed to fade from sight, as did the unsettling trees, which had only become gigantic as the nightmare unfolded. The blackness was now inside him. It whispered, faintly, then, more audible. It was of a foreign tongue, yet Besnard could somehow understand the twisted language. *"Hoallawth scheeh wa beelza meype.....beelza sata shay meype".* "Come to me my child....as my child comes home."

Besnard couldn't hear the rain, nor the wind or the horse or feel his pounding heart. He shut his eyes and lay back on the steed. He let go and let the monster inside take him.

He felt sweat grinding against more sweat as his head slammed into the horse's large skull. His own head was jerked to the right then whipped back. He slowly opened his eyes, not because he wanted to but because he was acutely aware that light; very bright, unusual light now faced him. The wind and thunder roared again, now louder than before. Besnard was soaked. He shivered. He was starving.

He had arrived.

The Commons was not as it should be. There were no rowdy crowds, no magistrate, sheriff or jailer. The usual assortment of beggars with their missing limbs and teeth had stayed away. Even the few mercurial wolfhounds that kept the gawkers safe were absent. Besnard could only wish to wake. Perhaps the drink had had its way. The *poitín* that came from his neighbour Gearoid's stillhouse might have been a little too robust for the taking.

But he knew he wasn't asleep and he certainly wasn't drunk. He knew this was all very real. There was no shutting it out or disappearing softly into a lukewarm state of denial. He was here, in the place where he had slipped the noose around hundreds of heads, released the rope and heard necks crack, seen eyes bulge, watched blood turn purple then black, and watched bad, sick people die. He was here where no one else was.

Except the man in the noose in the blinding storm light.

The light was coming from the *Bean Si Sisters*. They were a pair of almost identical blackthorn trees, directly in the centre of The Commons, with a circular clearing surrounding them. Locals said it was a fairy fort or perhaps a druid's sacrificial mound. *But it was a cracker of a place to hang people.* Blackthorn is very strong. It does not bend easy. And the view was like a theatre in the round; everyone got a good look.

Besnard stumbled down from his horse. His legs wobbling as he shuffled towards the glow. Squinting, he vomited in his mouth, swallowed, and then regurgitated the entire mess onto his boots. Bent over, with icy rain slashing his bare head, he slowly looked again at the trees.

There was a man, that was clear, although one of great stature. He towered above the useless executioner, no less than eight foot high. His arms and legs were long, thin and twisted. His hair, like the knotted tails of a rat-king made up of a hundred panicked beasts.

He was dark. He was awful darkness. He was a terrible deep blackness that could only come from one place.

Hell.

Besnard thought he *must* be there. Where else could he be?

The horrible thing in the noose had no other discernible features except two eyes that were the colour of a bluish purple seen in dead flesh and a scaled tongue that was reddish-pink and bifurcated. The tongue lashed out from the area where the neck should have been and began to move up and down, undulating rhythmically, in between large drops of rain and forceful windy gusts.

"Oh Jesus..." whispered Besnard, as he felt the ground meet his knees.

The tongue was now ten feet from the source, still pulsating, moist and serpentine in movement. Besnard's breathing was shallow, his heart, pounding. He was crying and could not stop. He desperately wanted to say his Act of Contrition but could only think it:

"My God....I...I am sorry...for... for my sins.....with all my heart.......in...in choosing to to do wrong........ and failing..... failing....failing to do good...I......I....have.... sinned...... against You...You ...you..whom...whom...wh......"

There was more to it yet Besnard couldn't finish.

He could not continue because another was uttering the prayer *out loud*. The tone was seductive. It had a hiss to it, sounding shrill. It mocked him, devouring his last hope:

"......whom I should love........above all things..... I firmly intend....with Your help, to do penance, to sin no more, and to avoid whatever leads me..... to sin...".

The man in the noose was laughing as the tongue now gently snaked its way along the back of Besnard's neck, across his throat and then looped around and around.

Seven times.

#NoFilter
by Alexandra Graves

I have always despised waking up really early in the morning. There are exceptions, though. Once in a while I get up unusually early for one reason or another, and I find that I actually like it. I realized this was one of those days as I pulled into the gravel parking lot. When I looked straight ahead past my windshield all I could see were rows upon rows of trees– I loved it. I quickly grabbed by camera bag, notebook, chapstick, and a pair of gloves because it was still chilly out, and then I was ready to get a move on.

When I stepped off of the concrete and onto the trail I quickly began to realize that it rained heavily in the mountains the night before. The black sole of my running shoe was squishing into the mud and kicking up pieces of dirt with every step. I took in a deep breath once I got onto the trail, and the forest air smelled as though it was laced with traces of mud and punctuated by the scent of damp leaves. I could see the sun hovering just above the horizon. The golden light extended into graceful linear streams, slicing through the greenery. This view was one of the main reasons for my early morning walk. It was breathtaking.

When I got to the edge of Mud Lake I noticed that someone was already there. I could see a man in a red jacket sitting on some large rocks near the water's edge. I thought this was a little bit odd because it was 5:50 in the morning on a Tuesday, but I didn't give it much thought; I had an assignment to do. I found a log to sit on a good distance away from the man, maybe 15 feet. This would be a good place to write and take pictures for my photojournalism class, I thought. After a few moments of taking notes on my surroundings, I noticed the man break his gaze across the lake. He hadn't moved much since I sat down. I could see in my peripheral vision that he turned to face me.

"What're you doing awake so ungodly early for?" he asked. The man's face was expressionless, flat. His tone was contrastingly friendly. It was a strange paradox I couldn't quite grasp (especially that ungodly early in the morning).

"I came out here for a school assignment," I replied. "I wanted to take some photos of the forest at dawn and get some inspiration for my short story."

"You a photography student?"

"No, journalism," I replied. "It's for a photojournalism class I'm taking this semester," turning my attention back to my notebook. After a moment, I looked up at him and asked, "You were here before me – what brought you here so early?"

He paused, turned to me and replied, "That's a long story." Then he let out an audible sigh. His attention suddenly seemed to be elsewhere again.

"I'm a good listener," I volunteered.

He seemed to contemplate that for a moment, and then he stood up; he was easily over six feet tall. A rumpled and faded red jacket covered his broad shoulders. He walked over and sat next to me. His eyes, framed by several lines and creases, were grey with flecks of blue. They were wide and friendly.

"My wife and I used to hike these trails near Mud Lake. She

passed twenty years ago."

"Oh. These trails are beautiful; I can see why you two would have enjoyed it here. What was your wife's name?"

"Her name *is* Sophie... I like to come early in the morning to see the sun rise. It's quiet, and it gives me a chance to just sit and remember her. Although today, I'm happy to have a little company."

He looked down at his hands for a few moments, back into his thoughts again. I wasn't expecting to discuss such a heavy topic, especially with someone who I had just met. I began to feel heavyhearted, but I didn't know how to respond in that moment. I'm terrible at filling silences.

"When Sophie and I met we were both a few months shy of our college graduation, so neither of us really had any spending money. I couldn't take her anywhere nice. She sure was special to me, though. Lucky for me she liked the outdoors. We both appreciated nature, and these walks were our little escape from our lives. On our first few dates we just walked and talked... today is our forty-second anniversary."

Sometimes you can see a person's feelings written all over their face. The man turned into an open book when he started talking about his wife. He was facing me, but he wasn't seeing me – his mind's eye was taking him to a place far into the corners of his memory.

He continued after a brief pause, changing gears.

"Our relationship was anything but easy. No one tells you how hard it is sometimes. Most people only talk about the good things, and they hide away the hard times. It wasn't easy but we made it work, by working hard at it. When Sophie and I were in our mid-twenties we broke up and got back together every other day. You fight, you hate each other sometimes, but if it's worth it to ya you'll stick it out. That's the only way it will work. You're still figuring out who you are in your twenties – remember that. Don't take every little thing too seriously; the world will keep on spinning even when you think something so terrible has happened that your life is over. It's not."

He paused, thought some more. He stood up and took his wallet out of his pocket, and then he sat back down beside me.

"This is our little girl, Chelsea. She's not so little anymore, hey?"

The woman in the photo looked like she was in her mid-thirties. She wore very little makeup, and she had a wide, warm smile just like her dad.

"She's living in Toronto now, got a job over there at a law firm. I don't get to see her often enough, but she still calls every few days. I worry that she only calls that much because she feels like she needs to check in on me. I don't want her to worry. I'm doing just fine. Got the dog, I have my friends and my hobbies, I keep busy."

"Your daughter must have got her good looks from her mom," I joked. Then I switched gears too. "Twenty years is a long time – did you ever remarry after Sophie?"

"Haha," he chuckled. "Not a chance, my dear. That woman took my heart with her to the grave. None left for no one else."

—

The man's name was Carl Jenkins. We talked for another forty minutes or so before we said goodbye. We exchanged contact information via Facebook (yes, he has Facebook), and I can proudly say I became his 86th friend.

Perhaps, I thought as I walked back to my car, this interaction was so poignant for me because of how raw and unexpected it was. My generation has the power to literally filter away any blemish, and choose to post only the best moments without context. We keep up with our social sphere by liking photos of our friends when they show us what they what us to see. Whereas with Carl, I felt like I got a miniature glimpse into his universe, his pain, and his happiness. It was...genuine. We really do filter our reality for others to a degree that society has never seen before.

It's fair to say I didn't capture any pictures of the forest while the sun was rising. Instead, I walked back to my car with a little more warmth in my heart than I had before.

Carl shared his hardship, but he didn't share a sob story. He wasn't unloading his feelings on me as a means to seek comfort. Instead, he shared his story, the good and the bad. His love, their fights, her illness, and how he's moved on without finding someone to fill the void. Perhaps there wasn't a void to speak of, as Sophie clearly lived on in his mind. I'm not saying that this is the right way for everyone to deal with loss, but I think it was the only way that was right for him. He was strong in his convictions; he knew how he felt. Carl didn't filter the ugly parts of his life, and the contrast – his authenticity – made him shine a little brighter. This is kind of the way I feel about this muddy trail, and the lake presumably named after it. It's a little messy, but beautiful.

Terminal

by JD Lyonhart

Fred: We're the true victims of 9/11.

Thomas: Don't.

Fred: It's just math.

Thomas: Please. Not in an airport.

Fred: No, seriously. How long have we been waiting? And we've had to lug our bags around the whole bloody time. It's insane. How many people do you think go through these lines every day?

Thomas: I don't know.

Fred: Would you say at least 50,000?

Thomas: Sure.

Fred: So what's 50,000 times 365 days a year?

Thomas: I don't know. I'll check my phone...

Fred: It's 18 million.

Thomas: So you've done this before?

Fred: And after 9/11 they beefed up security. More security, more lines, more probes. For the sake of argument, let's say 9/11 increased wait times by 10 minutes per person. Now, what's 10 minutes times 18 million people?

Thomas: 180 million minutes.

Fred: And that's just one airport. You times that by 50 states, and you get?

Thomas: Just tell me.

Fred: No. Guess.

Thomas: I don't know. Billions.

Fred: Exactly.

Thomas: Not exactly. I just estimated. That's the exact opposite of exactly.

Fred: It's 9 billion if you want to be a dingus about it. Times that by the years since 9/11, and you get 140 billion minutes. And do you know how many minutes the average life is?

Thomas: Including the aborted ones?

Fred: 40 million minutes. Take the number of minutes wasted and divide it by the average life span, and you know how many lives have ended in these lines?

Thomas: Including the aborted ones?

Fred: You're hilarious. It's 3500 lives. Way more than 9/11. And that's just American airports. If you factor in like Canada, that's another say, 50 lives. Which means–

Thomas: –that you've never been to Canada?

Fred: –that we are the true victims of 9/11.

Thomas: Of course. That was my second guess.

Fred: You and me and the hot chick in front of us are the true casualties of 9/11. Plus, you know, Iraq...

Thomas: How noble of you to think of Iraqi children in the midst of your struggle.

Fred: Thank you. And now for my point.

Thomas: Oh God.

Fred: We spend most of our lives waiting for things; waiting till summer, waiting till Christmas, waiting till were old enough to get laid–

Thomas: –now I see why you care about this–

Fred: –waiting till we get the right job, waiting till you find the one, waiting till you have more time, waiting, waiting, waiting, and, wait for it, more waiting.

Thomas: Complaining doesn't make it go any faster.

Fred: Oh, I'm not complaining. I'm just pointing out the ridiculousness of it all.

Thomas: That doesn't change anything either.

Fred: I don't want to change it. My problem isn't the

wait times; it's the time we spend waiting.

Thomas: ...

Fred: Life isn't about the destination; it's about the journey. It doesn't matter where you're going, only that you enjoy the ride. Haven't you seen any movie ever? If we stopped looking forward in anticipation and just existed in the present, then every moment would be valuable in and of itself, and not just for the inevitable, deterministic future it's heading towards.

Thomas: Ok, but if you just live in the moment you screw over the future. Global warming and the economic crisis and the treaty of Versailles are basically your theory put into colossally crappy practice.

Fred: I'm gonna take that last point as a covert appeal to Hitler and just ignore it.

Thomas: And I bet you half the people in this line have issues 'cause their daddy chose the heat of the moment with some chick in a bar over their families' long-term future. And what about delayed gratification?

Fred: Like...sexually?

Thomas No, perv. They did a study with some kids. They told them they could either have one cookie now or two cookies later. The kids who waited were more successful later in life.

Fred: What's success though? Becoming a working stiff who's too concerned with where they're going to enjoy the ride?

Thomas: But it's not an either/or. Of course you shouldn't waste your life waiting for the future, but you also shouldn't screw over your and everyone else's future by just indulging whatever whims you have in the moment. There's a balance. You can enjoy the ride while still making sure you're riding in the right direction.

Fred: Theoretically, yeah. But most of us spend so long figuring out where we're going that we don't have time to enjoy the ride. We're so busy checking the map that we forget to check out the scenery.

Thomas: True. But if you get too distracted by the view you crash into a telephone pole.

Fred: Do they still have telephone poles?

Thomas: Ok, a Seven-Eleven or something.

Fred: Do they still have Seven-Elevens?

Thomas: The point is you die.

Fred: Gonna die either way. But your way you spend your whole life waiting to live; waiting till you get married, waiting till you get that promotion, waiting till you can retire, and then *bam*! End of the line.

Thomas: And what's at the end of the line?

Fred: Nothing.

Thomas: But if the point of your whole little manifesto is that life is purgatory, then what's next?

Fred: Who cares?

Thomas: I care. I enjoy thinking about life and death and all that crap. That doesn't distract me from the joy of the moment, that brings me joy in the moment.

Fred: And that's why you're so boring at parties.

Thomas: See, I actually find that people who just live in the moment are the ones most boring to spend a moment with. They've got no depth, just ejaculatory urges that leave the person next to them unsatisfied. It's all climax all the time; no foreplay, no rising action, no character development. It's fun in college but it's depressing everywhere else.

Fred: Oh come on, chill out a bit – you're not going to hell for having a little fun.

Thomas: You don't know that.

Fred: Seriously?

Thomas: I didn't say it's true. Just that you don't know that it isn't.

Fred: Um, torture and fire and little red demon men... that's what you want to believe?

Thomas: I don't *want* to. But there are lots of things I don't like that are still real.

Fred: Jesus Christ! You're like a pharaoh wasting your whole life decorating your tomb.

Thomas: Ha. Then you're a centurion building an empire that will inevitably fall to dust.

Fred: At least I'll get to fiddle while the world burns. Even Nero got in a glorious decade before it all went to hell.

Thomas: Common. You're not even a little scared of death?

Fred: Why? I'm not gonna be there for it.

Thomas: See, everyone says that when things are good but no one means it when it actually counts. Can you honestly tell me you've never thought about it? Not even as a kid?

Fred: Maybe at like 3 AM when I'm alone and had too many Red Bulls. But there's too much going on in this world to worry about an imaginary future beyond it. I'd rather take the cookie I can see than the two I can't.

Thomas: But what if you spend your whole life going down one road, only to get to the end of it and realize you were heading in the wrong direction all along?

Fred: What if aliens destroy the world tomorrow? You could ask 'what if' about anything; all we really know for sure is today. Eat, drink and be merry. YOLO. Life is a highway. Live long and prosper. Party like there's no tomorrow. Enjoy the ride. Need I go on?

Thomas: But there's no 'what if' about it. Every road ends. You can only live in the moment so long until you're out of moments.

Fred: Exactly! It's precisely because life is short that you have to go all out, devour every second, milk the world for all it's worth.

Thomas: 'What good is it to gain the whole world but lose your soul?' Do you know who said that?

Fred: David Bowie? Just promise me you won't become one of those religious nutters who's so busy waiting for heaven that they're no earthly good.

Thomas: But heaven and earth are not mutually exclusive. It's not either/or. It's both!

Fred: How? How is it both?

Thomas: Because shouldn't contemplating heaven make you better here and now? I mean if you're constantly thinking about a place of love and peace and joy, how can that not trickle down into your life on earth?

Fred: But that's not what religious people are thinking about! They're thinking about gated mansions and streets of gold. A place where there are rainbows but no gay people. A place with infinite Chinese buffets but no foreigners. A place where there are no abortions because there are no women; just white males in an eternal circle jerk. Put that on a necklace.

Thomas: Ok, granted. Crappy people on earth have a crappy view of heaven. But shouldn't that same logic show that if someone had a better view of heaven they might just be better on earth as well? Have you seen Les Mis?

Fred: Which one? Liam Neeson or Hugh Jackman?

Thomas: Jackman. The part at the end where he goes to heaven; where everyone's standing victorious on the barricade; where Jean Valjean is reunited with Fantine; where the world is turned upside down and now the peasants are on top; where the revolution actually succeeded and tyranny is overthrown and things are the way...things were meant to be.

Fred: Fairy tales.

Thomas: But fairy tales give us hope!

Fred: False hope.

Thomas: Why is it false?

Fred: Because it's too good to be true.

Thomas: Um, ice cream, puppies, blowjobs, Netflix? Just because something's awesome doesn't mean it's not real.

Fred: First of all, I'm lactose intolerant. Second, Netflix stole three years of my life, and third, um, when was the last time you got a blowjob?

Thomas: 2014. Or 2013. It was New Year's Eve so–

Fred: –I will, however, concede puppies. But that's all I will concede. Heaven is just too rich to indulge, it is the epitome of wishful thinking.

Thomas: So hell isn't real because you don't like it, and heaven isn't real because you like it too much?

Fred: I know you don't actually believe all this, so what are you doing? Heaven doesn't need a devil's advocate.

Thomas: I don't know. I just think that how you see the future impacts how you live in the present. Whether that's heaven or just your goals or dreams or whatever. So if you think after death there is nothing, what can stop that nothingness creeping in?

Fred: What does that even mean?

Thomas: Like, remember that movie *Children of Men* where women can't have babies anymore? The whole world goes to crap, because there's no future.

Fred: It's just a movie, man.

Thomas: No, it's not. It's history in a nutshell. A society's picture of the future has always been linked to how it lives here and now. What you long after, what you strive for, that's what you become. We are our hopes.

Fred: That's not history! That's just your, your... personal musings!

Thomas: No it's not! I mean, just look at the last hundred years. We got so obsessed with progress and machines and our bright scientific future that we used science to gas, gun and grenade the hell out of the present. We split the atom and the pieces went everywhere.

Fred: Exactly! Every nation was so preoccupied with the future and greedily getting what they wanted out of it that they lost sight of what they already had here and now. That's why surfers make shitty soldiers; they're too busy living in the moment to fight for the future.

Thomas: Surfers make shitty soldiers?

Fred: And if you want to talk about heaven, let's talk about heaven. If heaven existed, it would be full of people like me basking in the glory of the moment, while everyone else would be so focused on the future that their present would feel like hell. Every day they will be forced to make plans in a notebook, and at the end of the day it will all be erased and they will start over again. They will be sentenced to forever walk down a beautiful road that they will never enjoy, because they will be too focused on their destination to stop and look around them at the–

Airline Attendant: –Hello, please step forward sir with your passport out and open to the picture.

Fred: Hi. Yeah, here.

Airline Attendant: Thank you. Just one second please...Oh...am I correct that your end destination is Chicago?

Fred: Yes.

Airline Attendant: I'm sorry to inform you sir, but this is the wrong line.

Fred: What? You're kiddin' me! We've been waiting here for nearly an hour and our flights already boarding.

Airline Attendant: I'm sorry, sir. The line for domestic flights is, in fact, in the domestic wing of the airport.

Thomas: Well Fred, at least we had a good time waiting in line.

Fred: Oh fuck off.

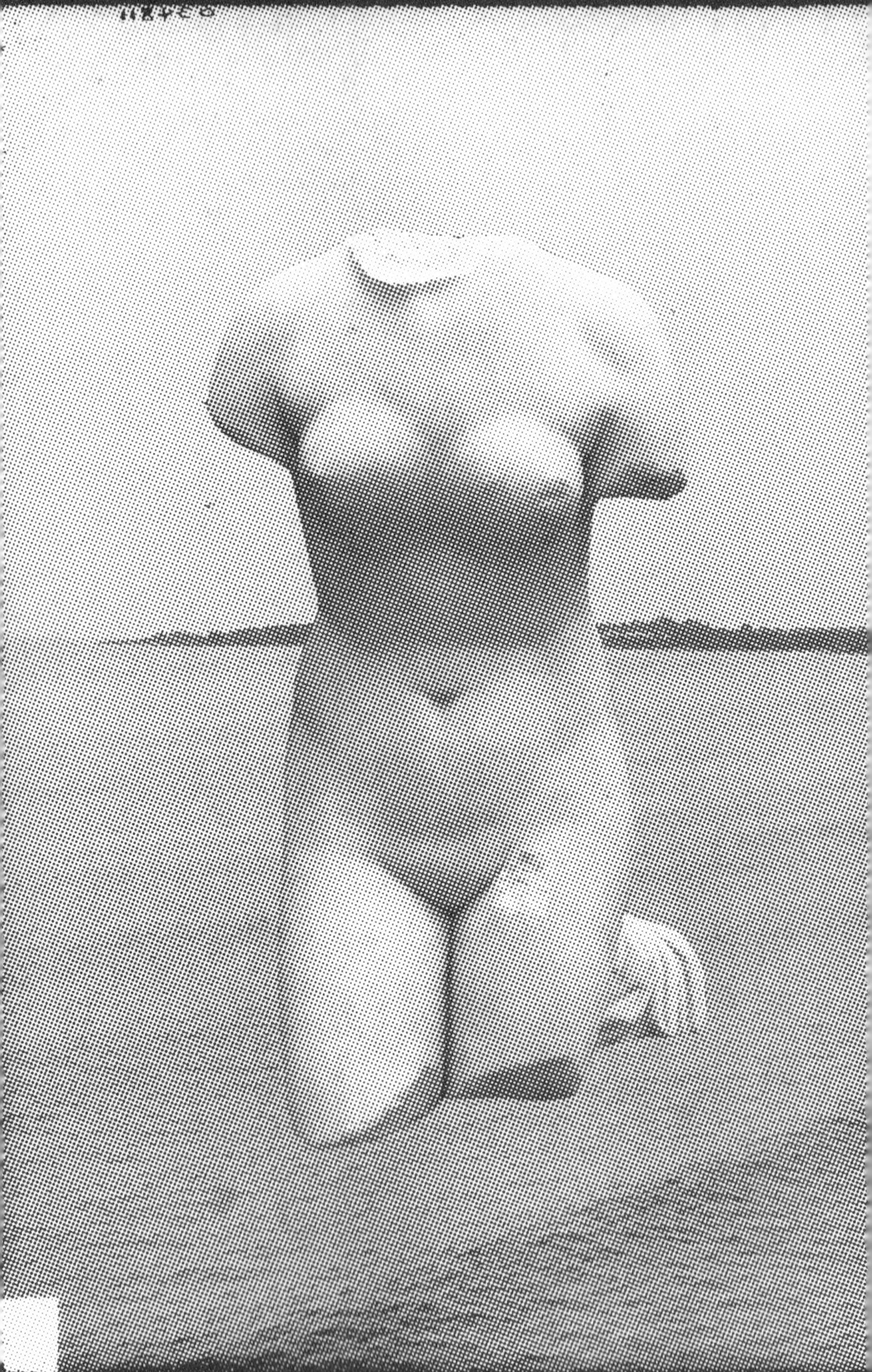

Tits

by JD Lyonhart

A man was going down to Jericho Beach when he saw a woman slumped against the side of a tower asleep. Wild hair twirled around the unkempt kernel of her former face, perched atop bones shed of any real jelly. She was still alive, but had that stickish look that insects have, as if at any moment she would crack and crunch from the mere tug of gravity. She must have dozed off while begging, for her left arm had slid down, towing her bra, exposing breasts too pale to belong to such decrepity. And the nipple. There was definitely a fugitive nipple poking out, reaching up for the sun.

What injustice! He spat to himself. Here she lies, sprawled out on rich tile, while above her evil schemes cling and clang about, bureaucratic bastards in their castle in the clouds. His pace increased to match his verbiage. Capital stolen in the capital city, girls debauched and left for dead on the side of the road, while their only road home is an urn. Wealthy pricks dancing about their shops, while an ancient skeleton burrows up out of the cement. How Western, how medieval, how bourgeoisie, how blind the masses of men?

By the time his wrath had been sufficiently sated, he'd gone so far away from the girl that he could no longer do anything for her, staring back at that starving speed bump a few blocks ago. He didn't think it was possible, but she looked even less significant now, shrunk and shrivelled by an inconvenient distance. Then again, he thought to himself, who am I to question her life choices? Ha! me? her patron!? her male savior?!? Perhaps this is the life she wants, the lone ant fleeing the anthill before the coming of the magnifying glass. She is like Marianne going bare breasted over the barricade, proclaiming liberty to the manacled masses, those slaves of a stuffy office, tossed about by the good tidings of the tide and the high seas of stuff. Unshackled from the oven and the desk, she alone was free to sit, to skip, to sell, to buy, to live, to kill, to die. A woman's Walden!

His heart and step a little lighter, he continued on with his day, comforted in the knowledge that it wasn't really him who'd helped her, but she who'd helped him.

Soon, another man passed by on his way to Jericho Beach. He saw the girl and she sawed his heart in two, reminding him of his sister.

Thud! He dropped his beach chair to the ground in shock. Without a second to waste, he ran into McDonald's, buying her a meal, supersizing the coffee and getting a second hash brown to boot. He nearly spilt the coffee rushing to return, and then placed the feast at her feet. She didn't gobble it up but retained all the manners of whatever past hung about in her head. Then he helped her up, bought her new clothes, and helped her find a job in a grocery store, meeting all her material needs.

Two weeks later the sun was out again with a smile, and so–chair in hand–that man marched himself back down to Jericho Beach. *Thud*! There she was again! She was bloody well back with her bloody back against the wall. He soon pried out that she loved her pimp, and wouldn't leave him. He was the only one in the whole world who cared for her, she said. The only one who protected her from bad men. Her body might have been fed but her soul was still empty, craving the affirmations of the crass and identities she'd dropped in the gutter.

The man stormed off, exhausted of trying to help such try-ing people. He could be heard for years after off in the dis-tance, lecturing whoever dared drop a coin in a homeless hat; "They're just using you for booze and cigarettes, man."

Finally, another fellow walked past on his way down to Jeri-cho Beach. He was tanned head to toe, except for a white splotch on his neck, where the sun seemed to have baked around a cross necklace. His long hair reminded everyone of the messiah he worshipped, falling into his eyes as he kneeled down to the girl's level. He wielded the knowledge that she was loved *by* love, a passion so bold it would lay down its life, infinity proposing to her in the streets. He had within him the good news that all ungodded gutters could be made divine again, that even if her little legs couldn't climb to heaven she could still be scooped up by the arms of eternity, repatriated to paradise. Yet with all the joy and hope of two thousand years in his arsenal, the man kneeled down, reached out his hand, hurriedly covered her exposed breast, and left.

Her fully clothed corpse was not discovered dead till many hours after the fact, the perfume of her profession covering over the initial rigors of mortis. People only noticed she'd died when a bird plucked out her eyes, dripping them up over the buildings, eyes rolling from the treetops, glaring down at us all.

Trump Sparks
War With CBS

by JD Lyonhart

President Trump's war with Hollywood continued Monday night, firing back at CBS regarding one of its most popular shows.

"It's propaganda, folks. Liberal propaganda. You see it every day on television. And it's sad. I really think it's tragic. This show is glorifying an illegal immigrant, an illegal immigrant who contributes nothing to society, nothing I can tell, just stays up late in a nightclub. And he's a main character. Not a side character. Main character."

These comments followed on the heels of his statement in Playboy Magazine the previous month:

"This show's gotta go. It's black and white. They've got this loud-mouthed, obnoxious, Rosie O'Donnell wannabe type. She's loud, obnoxious, doesn't work a job–a real MacGillicuddy–just sits at home getting money from taxpayers and her husband. And it's got a horrible message, no moral compass at all, that I can tell ya. The main couple never even sleeps in the same bed at night."

The public has jumped on the insensitive comparison, noting that it has only been a few weeks since O'Donnell's alleged suicide. Yet Trump continued unabated, furthering his critique of the show via Twitter at 2:38am:

"Worse every week. Stealin from cities, disrupting trains, shutting down a factory, mocking John Wayne! GROW UP! #MakeAmericaGreatAgain"

Later in the day, Dr. Trump (honorary PHD, St. Petersburg University) gave an impromptu lecture at NYU, shocking students and teachers alike when he made an appearance in Architecture 202. He was quoted as saying:

"Indiana Jones would never have gotten away with this in the 80's, believe me, that I can tell you. The people miss the good ole days of television. They should. That's what we're gonna get back to. I promise you that."

As of 10:30pm tonight, no one at the *I Love Lucy* show could be reached for comment.

THE DOOR
IS
ALWAYS
OPEN.

3rd Corinthians

by JD Lyonhart

To the church in Corinth,

Grace and peace to you from God our Father and the Lord
Jesus Christ.

It is actually said among the people that you will not take
in the Roman Christians and Jews. Indeed, since Emperor
Claudius banished them from Rome, you have made it your
duty to deny such exiles and applauded anyone who followed
in your shame. Families are fleeing for their lives, yet none
have found refuge with you in Corinth. At first I did not wish
to write you, knowing as I did your many struggles, not wish-
ing to burden you with more. Alas, last night I had a dream
that rebuked me from my slumber. In my vision a howl came
from a wounded mutt, running from the woods, fleeing a
beast with legs like tree trunks and extra heads where ears
should be. The mutt ran from home to home, whimpering
for someone to let him in. Yet door after door closed, until
he was left all alone in the dark to be consumed by the beast.

Perhaps you do not understand. Perhaps you do not see the
tears turning old trails to mud, nor smell the blood collecting in flesh-clogged gutters, nor hear the howl of brothers
and sisters climbing over each other to escape. I prayed as
much, for ignorance can be corrected by the Logos of time
and study. But I fear your symptoms bespeak a different dis-

ease, one deeper than joints and bones and marrow. A demon lives among you.

I prayed that perhaps this was not so, that Corinth was sheltered from the flight of the innocent, and so was innocent itself. Alas, Corinth is on the coast. Have you not then become fishers of men, catching corpses in your nets, the thousands lost at sea as they flee Rome? Does it not make a faint sound, when your ships cascade through rising and falling skulls on the tide? Have your homes not moved further inland, as the Mediterranean rises, displaced by death? Do you think yourselves merely lost in the Red Sea, whilst swimming in blood? Indeed, you are right in this at least: you are lost. Bodies float onto your beaches, yet you are the ones who are washed up.

One day, not long from now, you shall wake up not in your beds but at the pearly gates, howling at the door. Will you be taken in? Indeed, what excuse shall you give your Lord then? Shall you stand before the all-knowing Spirit and claim: "We did not know!" Will you stand before the one who taught us to love our neighbor, and say: "They were not my neighbor, for they did not live in my neighborhood, but in another town, far away." Will you stand before the one who paid the ultimate price for you, and mumble: "It would've cost too much to save them." Will you dare stand before the crucified Christ, and argue: "Rome would have killed us if we helped them."

So what if some of them might be spies of the empire? So what if they might bring terror and plague? Would it not be better to die for their humanity than to live and lose your own? What did you expect – that love would not cost everything? That following a crucified Christ might not mean you too would be crucified? If you want wealth and privilege and the promise of safety, then go worship Zeus or Artemis. If you want to follow Christ, then pick up your cross daily, dying yourself so others can live. The symbol of our faith is not gold or lions or lightning. Nay, it is death. A lover's death.

Do you not remember? Have you forgotten so quickly? Indeed, it has only been a few decades, many of you were there yourself, and for those who weren't, my friend Luke has documented the whole event. Remember those first days after Christ was crucified? When the authorities in Jerusalem began to hunt you down and slaughter the disciples? The government claimed we were traitors, just like our leader who was crucified for rebellion. You all fled North toward the land of Syria. You all took refuge there, hiding until it was safe. If the people there had not embraced you, sheltered you, fed you, then all of us would have died, and the movement would have died with us. All Christians from the beginning through to the end of time, are, were and ever shall be, Syrian refugees.

I, Paul, write this with my own hand.

The grace and peace of our Lord be with you. My love to all of you in Christ Jesus.

Amen.

A Housing Crisis
[On Infinite Earths]

by B.C. Woodruff

"And over here we have the master bedroom." Tania McMillian ushered the couple through the door, pausing them in front of the demonstration king-size bed. The window, facing east, showed a bright sun crowning above a neighbouring building across the river. The room wasn't large, but the pale blue paint gave it a depth that worked in its favour.

Pauleen Colt and her fiancé Timothy Prince took in the scene, wandering around the bed and then down the short hall of closets to the ensuite bathroom. There, Timothy stopped, turned around, and shook his head.

"I dunno, Pauly. I liked that last one better..."

"I know you did. So did I, honestly. It was just too far out of our budget. We have to be careful about where our finances are going these days, remember?" She rubbed the small bump below her pink camisole.

"I know... but..."

Tania took the opportunity to leap in. "I'm sure we'll find you a unit here that fits your needs and your means. Alvana Corporation is always ready to go the extra step to help our clients find the right home." She smiled and her teeth literally twinkled. Lighteeth had become rather popular among Alvana's sales teams, though the novelty seemed to be wearing thin on people. Particularly on Pauleen, who had just enough patience and just enough foresight to force a blink as her realtor's mouth began to widen.

"What other models do you have on this foundation? We really like the location"– Pauly turned to Timothy–"isn't that right, *dear*?"

"Sure. Fine. You're right," Timothy said.

Tania nodded. "We have two more units available in Adjuncts." She tapped on her temple and projected a screen from a small piece of tech mounted above her left eyebrow. "That one over there is about 350 credits less than the one we're in now," Pauly noted, pointing past a hologram of a housing complex that was clearly beyond their budget. It was immense. Fifty, perhaps even sixty floors reaching up from an aerial tether foundation.

"*350 less*? How is that possible?" Timothy felt a strange mixture of excitement and confusion.

"It's located several dimes over." Tania concentrated and the housing complex faded away, replaced by an intricate web of lines with points, some red, some blue, and a few green. A note above one of the green dots read *You Are Here.*

"Let's take a look at one that's closer to your current place first. It'll only take a moment." Tania squinted and the display rearranged itself into a single line with all the green dots in order, shifting the blue and red ones into an unseen periphery. "Alright. So, here we are. As you've seen, it's a beautiful dimension. Nearly identical to the one you're both from. By law, I have to tell you that the one downside of this particular Earth is that due to a – wow, that's a lot of numbers. But yes, it says here that due to an approximately 0.0004% relativistic shift in particle velocity sometime around the formation of this dime's Solar System, you'll experience certain seasonal variations. Specifically in winter, which is a bit warmer. If you want specifics, well, we can talk about that later."

As she paused, Timothy cut in to help her get to the point. "Can we talk about the 350 credits cheaper model?"

"Right. So, if you look here…" The line in the projection slid over a few green dots to one near a grayed-out area. "This is a nice little dimension. Technically, I'm told, it's a *fractured* dimension that separated after the multiverse was in its 'cooling' phase."

"And why is it 300-odd less?" Pauleen asked.

"Oh, nothing too ridiculous. It's in a bit of a up-and-coming society. They've had some bad runs, these people. A couple world wars. The odd crusade or jihad here and there. But it's *mostly* harmless, especially if you pick one of the more developed countries."

Pauleen tapped her foot. It was a common sign that she was nervous, and Timothy wasted no time in patting her on the back. "Are there any predictive models that we can derive from neighbouring dimensions?" she asked. "Anything we can use to figure out where the world might be heading? And you said that it was 'up-and-coming' – what exactly do you mean by that?"

The realtor nodded, taking it all in. She had underestimated Pauleen, who clearly knew her stuff. "Lots of questions. Lots of questions… Hmmm. Alright, I can say this much based on another couple I sold a slice of land to in an area called England. They *love* it there. Once their dimensional realignment treatments finished up and they absorbed the local dialect and etiquette, they fit right in. Even plan to see if they can get their parents approved for extra-dimensional transition." Her voice fell to a whisper. "But they're *Prolytes*, so… I don't know if that's going to work out. But even so, I assure you that they're very happy with their decision."

"What about forecasting? We want to know what we'd be getting into."

This question made the realtor squirm a bit. "Like I said, it's *technically* a fracture, so we only able to make a superficial survey of the neighbours."

"And?"

Tania swallowed. "The neighbouring dimensions have succumbed to the Fermi Consequence." She coughed. "However! There's an above 90% chance that the fracture will avoid that eventuality."

"How can you be sure?"

"This particular fracture seems to be mending itself and re-integrating with the multiverse. It's rare, but not unheard of. If you're worried about any issues going forward, may I recommend getting causality insurance?"

"Hmmm." Pauleen seemed unconvinced. "And did you say *land* before? This place doesn't even have arcologies, then. It sounds awfully backward."

"It's not as bad as all that. I can take you to look at the unit there, if you like. We just need to go down to the transport. Won't take much more than an hour."

Timothy also looked frustrated. He opened his mouth to say something, but Pauleen got the floor first.

"It's so irritating that we've been entirely priced out of our home reality, you know? I mean, *we grew up there*! Then you have those massive trans-dimensionals sneaking in, speculating on all the good real estate, and... and... they don't even *live* here! There should be a tax... or... or *something*! I mean, have you seen how empty some of the cities are these days? You can't tell me that there isn't something just *wrong* about wandering around and seeing nothing but dark buildings at night. I can practically see the stars! Like, where's the light pollution? Where are all the *people*?! We wanted to raise our child somewhere affordable. We thought that would be where we grew up, but..." Pauleen took a corner of the bed, feeling dazed.

"But, I think she was saying, we have to look at other options. Now... I don't want to be insensitive here but... are there any *Prolytes* in this dimension?" Timothy flushed, embarrassed to have asked.

Tania nodded awkwardly.

"Yes, there are a *few* Prolytes. You simply can't get away from a population that dense as it expands through the multiverse. As you know, the Prolytean Dime is a mess. They've pretty much rendered their Earth uninhabitable. You have to understand that they..."

Timothy shook his head apologetically. "I didn't mean to be rude, really! I'm sorry. I just... I don't want to move somewhere and find that, suddenly, we're in the same position as we were at home." Timothy paced back and forth. Pauleen concentrated on the green dot ahead of her, imagining everything she could do with the commission – provided there was one in her future.

"Well... we could at least give it a look." She placed her hand on Tim's.

"You're right." He smiled to her and then turned to Tania.

"Lead on!"

Doesn't She Look Like Laura Moon?

by B.C. Woodruff

William is on the couch. He's crying, quietly. I want to walk over and hold him, tell him that everything is going to be fine. That he *can* beat this and that I will stand by him through it all.

I know this is a lie.

He's thirty-seven with thick gray hair that reaches down to his shoulders. It's ever-so-slightly curly, particularly at the ends. He has thin lips, and a complexion of rich, dark chocolate. He's a writer. A damn good one.

"I'll never write another word," he cries. "My creativity has been replaced by fear." His eyes are closed and I can see this is true.

I had one goal.

One task.

I blew it.

—

The conversation with the others is mercifully brief, taking up our usual place in the cellar of Rosaline's Diner out near the swamp. It's been abandoned since the late eighties and will continue in this fashion until it collapses on March 15th, 2019. The cause: a branch falling off from one of the lumbering trees creeping up around it, old and wise but rotted.

Frederick O'Hailey, one of the twelve in our group, is standing in the corner when I break the news that William has cancer.

"This was *precisely* the reason you were brought here!" he shouts, his voice deep and cold. "How? How did this happen?"

I tell him what William told me, that he used to go for secret cigarettes once I was asleep or when I was elsewhere. There was no way for me to prevent it. His addiction, somehow, was kept from me all the years we were together. I had William promise – and this I make sure to remind Frederick – that he would quit if we ever got married.

He lied to me.

Lied to me for eight years.

It cut me deeper than failure ever could.

"We *need* William to finish the story, Laura." He pauses and squeezes the bridge of his nose, concentrating. "Okay, okay, okay. We'll just have to encourage him to get further, and hope for the best."

He's talking about a book William is meant to start but never finish, a brilliant manuscript that, decades from now, will inspire groups across the country to rally against the government, inciting a series of violent counter-protests and brutal police actions... it doesn't end well for either side.

The power of words.

In the future we left behind, William never finished the book, and *this* is the heart of the conflict. Interpretation takes over. Imagination distills tantalizing ambiguity into brutal certitude. Thousands die in mere weeks, and the policies that follow in their wake create an even darker world.

Thus one man's unfinished dream steers the future into deep, turbulent waters.

"I'll... see what I can do," I tell Frederick before leaving the group to discuss their own redactions to the timeline, their successes against my failure. As encouraging as their progress has been, we've never had any illusions that any of our efforts will be worth a damn if I fail. If I could write it myself, take on the burden myself, I would – but the first and final law of our work is simple and savage: history must never remember us.

You might ask why we didn't take more drastic action. Goodness knows *I* did. But long before the project even started looking for recruits, researchers cloistered in dimly-lit rooms hammered out the principles that kept me from reciting the damned book from memory and being done with it, that prevented less subtle chrononauts from simply putting a bullet through the brain of the future's most brutal figures.

What they realized is that above all, history is *resilient*. Chalk it up to the zeitgeist, fate, or whatever you want – but once something happens, it tends to happen no matter how much force the future throws at it. Assassins' guns misfire, inspired lieutenants take up the cause in their leader's name, and history marches on. And for those that deal roughly with causality, time has little mercy. There are no second chances for people like us.

—

Back at home, I watch over William. I console him. Hold him. As a friend, as a wife, as a desperate muse. I wonder who would have been here in the original timeline. Would it have been his mother? Probably not. She lives too far away, and is old and frail besides. His sister? Possibly. The few times we've met over the years, Grace showed me nothing but welcome and warmth. But he might have just kept it to himself – and the pain that I see on his face makes me ache for the joy I once found there.

Has my influence on his life changed things?

Absolutely.

But we've been cautious, and the plan – all of our projections considered it sound.

But *this* wasn't part of the plan... and if things turn out worse than before, we'll never get another chance.

No matter how it happens, William will be dead by the end of the year. Not long from now. The last few months he'll have someone writing down his thoughts for him, having lost the energy to do it for himself. Perhaps this time around, that person will be me. Details like that don't matter much.

"I don't want to die," he whispers. "I... I wish I'd never started smoking."

I kiss him and pull away.

"You should *use* this energy. Use it to create something that will outlive us all."

His look of despair shifts, and his eyes begin searching my face, moving from side to side as though he's reading words printed there.

"Do you think I can beat this?"

"I do," I lie.

I feel him relax, his body slump.

"Can you get me my computer? I think I have more to write after all."

I try to focus on the mission and not the man in a slow state of decay in front of me. The man I've come to appreciate and admire. Have I also come to *love* him? There was so much training. So much preparation, with the stakes high and the need so great, that I wonder if I've allowed myself to lose track of what's *really* important. There's so little time left.

Instead of worrying, I allow myself to think *maybe I can make this work.*

His fingers come down on the keyboard and his face transforms into one of clarity, as if he's suddenly tapped into a wellspring of energy he'd never found before.

I step back and look over his shoulder...

And smile.

He's started it again.

Delight With Destruction
by B.C. Woodruff

[...]

I suppose you could say that I'm at least tangentially responsible. I *was* there for the inaugural testing and I *did* provide
the team with the resources to move forward in development.
But I can guarantee that my intentions were noble. I truly be-
lieved what we were doing would benefit humankind.

[...]

What was that?

[...]

Yes. I suppose I was... *aware* of that the technology might be
used irresponsibly, but I challenge you to name one revolution
that didn't cause at least a little chaos before the end. And if
you've actually *seen* the towers, heard the music of a thousand–

[...]

Yes. I'm sure you have. I don't disagree with what you're saying, exactly, but my conscience is clear. I'm not guilty of any
of the crimes you accuse me of.

[...]

Well, if you'll allow it, may I ask *you* a question? Why do you feel it is important to use this gift – and that's what this was meant to be, a gift – for these... purposes?

[...]

I hardly see what in heaven or Earth gives you the right to –

[...]

I *am* calm. I just know this is my only chance to –

[...]

Fine! But I'll need to start much closer to the beginning to argue my case. Is that acceptable?

[...]

Good. Now, when I was approached by Sanaatan Labs, I had only done enough investigation into their company to understand that their operating budget had been cobbled together from government contracts that were, shall we say, *difficult* to qualify for. Of course, when you've worked within the Mardox Initiative – don't bother looking it up, you won't find anything – you get a feel for when it's appropriate to simply *believe* what people are willing to tell you. Especially when it's a woman like Vishakha Malcolm. I suspect that even you have heard that name before. If not, allow me to provide you with some insight: by age eight, Vishakha was building her own radios and won the Euler Award for Mathematics, which involved solving an equation that had baffled the world for nearly two centuries. At *eight!* Can you imagine the intellect? The resolve? The discipline? She was the golden girl of Maths, but soon turned her interest to the world of engineering – first mechanical, then electrical, and rounded out with chemical. She graduated top of her class at Oxford before she was fifteen, completed her first doctorate by eighteen, and simultaneously founded companies to help impoverished children in her hometown and Sanaatan Laboratories.

[...]

Yes, I know there were some... unpleasant rumours about some of their... methods, but I urge you to remember that all we've accomplished is a reflection of that woman and her desire to *do good*.

[...]

I can't go any faster! Context is important.

[...]

I see. OK. Well, if you feel like you understand these events well enough, let me at least move up to my involvement in the project. I met V almost eight years ago in her home office in Liverpool. I was star-struck. Here was a woman that had done more in her twenty-six years than most people are likely to do in their lifetime – hell, even five reasonably remarkable lifetimes would probably fail to match her achievements. She was also very funny, making jokes and gentle puns while she introduced me to the nature of her new endeavour. If not for her good humour, I might have thought her mad, but V had a way of bringing lesser minds up to her level, if only for a moment, to see the most audacious concepts with incredible clarity. She wanted nothing less than to build a machine that could assess and map a person's consciousness, and to create a place for all such minds to live forever. She wanted it to be perfect. Her vision, as I said before, was altruistic. She wanted to ensure that the great minds of our generation and the ones that come after would be able to continue on, applying their intellect and their skills for the betterment of the world for as long as possible. And it worked.

[...]

When did your agents find their way into the project?

[...]

I apologize. I only asked for sake of curiosity. It seems likely that you would have had someone loyal to your cause laying the groundwork early on. Was it Richard? Was he the one that betrayed us? I always had a feeling about –

[...]

No need to shout. I'll continue. I was brought into the project to help coordinate the funding necessary to make the leap from prototypes into production. I have a bit of a knack for finding money from... unexpected sources. I'm known for my persuasiveness, and not without reason. And as you might imagine, Vishakha needed more than I'd ever gathered before. Billions. Now, when you move around a few million from a donor or two, practically no one bats an eye, but when you get into the figures we're talking about, well... you start receiving unexpected visitors. Governments, private interest groups, and I suppose I can't forget people like you – those that oppose our goals but proved perfectly content to pillage our work for their own purposes.

[...]

My apologies. I did say this was a gift, and I meant it, but we won't get anywhere arguing semantics like that. I only want you to understand that I wasn't working directly on the project. All I did was keep it funded and moving forward. Yes, I've seen the tower – as well as I could with that goggles-and-glove contraption at least – but I know there was never a place for me in it. In an empire of the mind, what need would there be for bankers like me? But I knew it could do such good. Imagine it! Virtual years passing in mere seconds for humanity's finest artists, scientists, and engineers. For every question, every crisis, there would always be time!

[...]

Ah. So we're done now, are we? Have I *offended* you somehow? I suppose I must have at some point, but I missed it. Was
it simply the money, I wonder? No, I suppose not – considering our security protocols, this operation of yours must have
been exorbitantly expensive.

[...]

Ah. I get it. We're just using it wrong. I had no idea I was
in the presence of such luminaries – the very gatekeepers of
mortality and the soul! I expect you'll try to burn the tower
down and cobble together a paradise of your own – the wor-
thy will have their rewards in perpetuity, and those that dare
to defy you will be cast into some fresh hell. I understand it
all! I assure you that with Vishakha dead, no matter what
programmers you have on your side, the tower will never fall
– and the sweetest heaven you build will lead your "chosen"
into madness. The mind can only take so much repetition!
You'll break even faster than –

[...]

Yes. Do it. Use the device! I'll gladly send my consciousness
into whatever horrors you have planned. It won't be *me*, anyway – just a copy. I'm surprised you didn't know that there's
no continuity between this side and the next. Do whatever
you want with my twin – I'm sure I'll be dead soon, anyway...

[...]

FINAL MEMORY SYNCED. UPLOAD COMPLETE. INITIATE
PROGRAM PURGATORY.

What... where... am I?

—

Time has lost all meaning – I might have only just arrived in this empty void, or humanity might have gone extinct millennia ago. All I know is that wherever I am – wherever this is – someone forgot to turn the machine off.

I drift here, utterly alone. There is no sleep. No companionship. No conversation other than my thoughts. They killed me after the interrogation, I'm sure. *Anima inviolatum*, they cried – the inviolate soul – right before using the project to shatter minds as they saw fit, to build a hollow heaven for a chosen few. I doubt they ever saw the irony.

But there are others like me.

I hear them through the silence, see them through darkness – at the very edge of thought, I know they are there.

We are shadows, yes, but we feel.

I feel.

I long for an end to the endless. For someone to find us.

To flip the switch.

But time has no meaning here.

So I wait, and I remember.

Echoes of Us

by B.C. Woodruff

"Can you believe this?" Orlan, my mentor and the Keeper of Rites from our tribe, moves his hands across the smooth, shimmering flesh of the stranger. "In all my years, I have *never* seen anything like this."

The Lingering Night is coming; days grow short, and there will only be a handful more before we pass into the next Abyssal Age. Those who fear the darkness have already begun their trek across the Bajtorn Bog towards the Empty Sea, where they will board the landships and follow the waning light, perhaps even to the sun-streaked plains where the Opal Dynasty still holds court. Though they may already be gone. So few of us survive. The world is no longer safe, if it ever was, and none from the lands near the Peak have ventured far since the Bright Era returned centuries ago.

We knew there would be deserters – there always are in these last days of light – but those who believe still in our principles stay. We guard the Great Mystery. It is our duty, our purpose, only to be revealed when all else ends.

So against our fear of the darkness, we have elected to stay and await the light.

"Did you hear me?" Orlan asks, giving me a tap on the shoulder.

"I'm sorry. I thought the sun would rise at the same time it did yesterday." My mind tends to wander at moments like this. The Keeper does not approve.

"Hmmm," he says, looking north. "Should be soon, I think. Do you see the line of light there on the horizon?"

I do, and I tell him so, forcing myself to be quiet again as he returns to examining the charred creature laying before us, wearing clothes unlike any I've seen or read about. We are fortunate, if it can be considered fortune, to finally have a flame to see by – a blazing stone shard, half-buried in the soil, that we've been following for the better part of a day since it fell from the sky. Whatever else was inside has burned or melted; this *thing* is all that escaped.

"Nothing like this has touched the earth since our ancestors emerged from the Land of Dreams within the City," he tells me as his hand moves over the creature's hairless head, circling the eyes, running over the bridge of the nose, and moving back and forth across the thick, ruby lips. All done without pity or revulsion.

I find Orlan's claim hard to believe.

The Keeper of Rites has access to the collective knowledge of all those who have come before him, thanks to the great binding. Each time he accesses the living archive of Keepers past, Orlan's own personality fades as his predecessors reawaken. They are cold. I've never liked them much.

"Keeper," I call him, as is common – there is only ever one Keeper, while classes such as mine are given numbers along with our titles. "Who... *What* is it?" Reluctant to touch this thing, I try to force him to tell me something he might not realize he knows.

He continues to move his hands over the creature, careful,

conscious, precise. Finally, he shakes his head, ending the trance. "I have no clue, Bearer," he says. He should call me Bearer Five, and would if we were in a more public location. I have another name, but it can only be spoken by loved ones.

Dousing the burning shard with dirt not thirty metres away, Bearers One through Four could turn around at any moment.

I want to call him by his true name, as I want him to call me by mine. But if we are caught there will be harsh punishments for both of us. It is likely, even as I sit here, that one of the Bearers will lodge a complaint that I am not adequately contributing to their efforts.

This will change after the matching ceremony later this year, when I will finally receive my calling. Before that time, however, I will stay close to the Keeper but keep my emotions in check, hoping I might learn something I can use during my matching to earn a place in the City of Glass.

"Surely, you must –"

Orlan has no interest in speculation. "Once I am confident I know what this is, I assure you that I will inform you of the discovery, Bearer Five."

It hurts to hear him use my full "name", but I ignore it and continue. "It looks... almost like us." I realize how obvious that sounds, but I can't help myself

"Right. Except..." He begins removing a small patch of charred clothing. It seems modesty is only for the living.

But it seems this visitor has no need of modesty.

"No genitalia. No..."

"*Orifice*," he interrupts, hoping to maintain decorum.

"Is it dead?"

He pauses from moving his fingers over it and places his head to the creature's chest.

"There is a faint beating. *Very* faint."

I can sense his concern. The Shamans will be arriving soon, and they could offer more insight – but by then, it might be too late. The sliver of light on the horizon has grown, nearly erupting, though we still remain in the shadow of Mount Ulysi.

"Something's happening," he declares, lifting his head from the creature's chest and stepping back. I take my leave of the Keeper to meet the other Bearers by the fire. They have done well, having almost subdued the flames. The shape of object within the blaze has become clearer, its edges charred but... familiar.

Bearer Four – a woman so like me we might be sisters – says, "It looks a great deal like the City of Glass, does it not? Only... much smaller." I nod, but my mind is already elsewhere. I've kept my thoughts about our parentage private, but it's difficult to stay silent. We may never know for sure, as only the Breeder who matches men and women can say for sure. Each of us grows up under a Nurturer's care, then a Teacher's watchful eye, and finally train under the Keeper. Some of us may yet become Mothers or Fathers ourselves, though I hope that this is not the case for me.

I wonder if Four has had similar thoughts.

Bearer Three, a man, nods.

The Keeper returns, finding his voice. "...the Avarice..." he says, considering the word and its impact. "...No. Not exactly. But similar. You know of the City of Sky, yes? A Keeper from long ago, Derra, found a similar fragment containing one of the Luminari."

"The Children of Light?" Bearer Two, another man, asks.

"Yes. But Keeper Derra's memories are vague on the subject. She said that the Luminari–"

The sunlight has reached us now, and as it washes over the creature, we watch it begin to glow and awaken.

"–Lived by the light. Drank it in. Consumed it and only it..." Keeper Orlan trails off as the Luminari turns towards us, bright and beautiful.

It tries to speak but its words are mere whispers – and though I can't understand it, the sound is wonderful in a way I can hardly describe. It burns to look at the Luminari, but I know we are in no danger. I sense neither fear nor panic, and I expect the Bearers and Orlan feel the same way. Above us, the sun is moving, cutting across the sky quickly enough to follow. In mere hours, it will vanish, and the darkness will return.

Without the sun's light, I'm certain the Luminari will die – here, at the peak of the world.

I wonder if there is anything we can do. Anything we could learn from the living dawn before night falls.

But all I find is doubt.

Sixth

by Ian Morgenheim

A long-awaited dream. Aline crouches at the cardboard terminal at Ferdinand and Main – it is an airstrip; all lights are
red; do not walk! – awaiting the sharp hiss of one of a dozen
idling jets. Spring Break, she feels, looking back as all compass directions say 'soon'. A soft breeze; arrector pili awake.
Time to live in a way none but the most imaginative smut
peddler could exploit. Windier still. Backpack (classic leath-
er-bottomed Jansport) carry-on checked, full, entirely legit.

The airplanes' din builds as enthusiastic applause. Clearly
she's doing something right, waiting away the reddening af-
ternoon at the corner terminal. Her left foot taps the rhythm
of anxiety; she sways.

Then the slow sweeping of six swords two blocks down –
Aline's plane. Two prop engines cradled by sharp blue wings,
trailing tendrils of blood-red feathers mere inches from Main.
In deference to a clear elder, the assembled jets stop milling
and back up gently, lining the opposite curbs, eight and eight
in apparent salute with engines cut to a tenth. The fleet drones
softly as the lucky liner approaches Terminal CB. Too slow
for Aline's nervous heart, but one cannot rush an old dance.

Finally, it arrives. Aline skitters down the wrapping-paper
tube to the unfurled, red-carpeted stairway to Up There.
Helpful phantom technicians flank her, take her arms and

arms, and we're in! "Ready, dear?" a voice asks, and Aline flashes the thumbs-up; up and away they fly, as promised.

The ascent describes the screw hung above the campus effigy not two hours prior. Wild vacationer Aline and the plane are being titered – pulled up through 50 cubic kilometers of air, leaves, and seeds of summer. Looking down: the orientation-era campus map, hers in living memory by day, every border a flowing dotted line. When will the door open? she wonders.

A crack of thunder; the siren sounds! A blood-red warning light spins above her. Four handholds grasped firmly – three, two, one – and the door bursts from its hinges. The hatch burns yellow, melts molten raindrops, falls ashen over her ad-opted home. Aline forgets to breathe, of course.

"Ready, dear?" the voice asks again, as if this is anything but reckless.

No answer necessary; skitter-step and the air is hers. She is ineffable Abraham, sixth spider Abraham, and she falls. She screeches into the night, chelicerae gladly achitter; falling, she sees her target – an ember-glowing dot at the edge of the world. Silk woven in older dreams perches at her back; it unfurls, freefall ends, and she sinks on the wind toward the smoldering tower as every elsewhere fades.

Abraham awaits the comfort of surface. A warm night, by hu-man standards, not unlike the summer shade from which she would hunt if she ate more than dream. Yet her prey smells *deli-cious*; any minute now and she will feast on the tower's secrets.

The moon rises behind Sixth Abraham; she is being watched by another sleeper. A blinding glare burns into her silken parachute. Panic. She casts a mile-wide shadow over the ember, mere stories below. Almost. Next time, no light. Next time.

A prayer to Seventh: keep whole; weave and be merry, for

tomorrow we die.

A flash of moonlight. Charred silk on the midnight breeze.

Caribbean blue wings. A trail of red feathers pierces the edge of her dream.

Aline awakens.

CONTRIBUTORS

Contributors

B.C. WOODRUFF

A writer and bibliophile with an appreciation for life, the universe, and nearly everything.

IAN MORGENHEIM

A lifelong love of gaming and a stroke of baffling luck led this writer and editor a third of the way across the world. Things have only gotten better since.

MATT EWART

Matt Ewart is an award winning screenwriter who studied at the Vancouver Film School and is actively working in the film industry as a writer and producer.

ALEXANDRA GRAVES

A 20-something writer living in Vancouver BC. When she's not writing she can be found enjoying the good things in life such as red wine, the outdoors, and world domination.

JP MC GLYNN

Born in Limerick, Ireland and raised in Ontario, this emerging author has stories to tell; not all of them glistening with a veneer of happy go lucky platitudes.

JD LYONHART

He is really just very happy to be here. Though a revolutionary at heart, his writings explore the paradoxes and absurdities of his own 'progressive' worldview. He is deeply confused, and wants others to realize how deeply they should be as well.

A WORK FROM SHATTER BOOKS

B.C. Woodruff

Ian Morgenheim

Matt Ewart

Alexandra Graves

JP McGlynn

JD Lyonhart

AN ANTHOLOGY